The Gatorboat Goof-up

By Sarah M. Hupp & John Fornof

Ribbits! is a creation of Bob Garner

Illustrated by Bernard Adnet

Zonderkidz

Zonder**kidz**.

The children's group of Zondervan

www.zonderkidz.com

The Gatorboat Goof-up
ISBN: 0-310-70566-5
Copyright © 2003 by Focus on the Family

Requests for information should be addressed to:
Zonderkidz, Grand Rapids, Michigan 49530

Editor: Barbara J. Scott
Interior Design & Art Direction: Laura M. Maitner

Printed in Singapore
03 04 05/TP/4 3 2 1

The truth will set you free.

John 8:32 NIrV

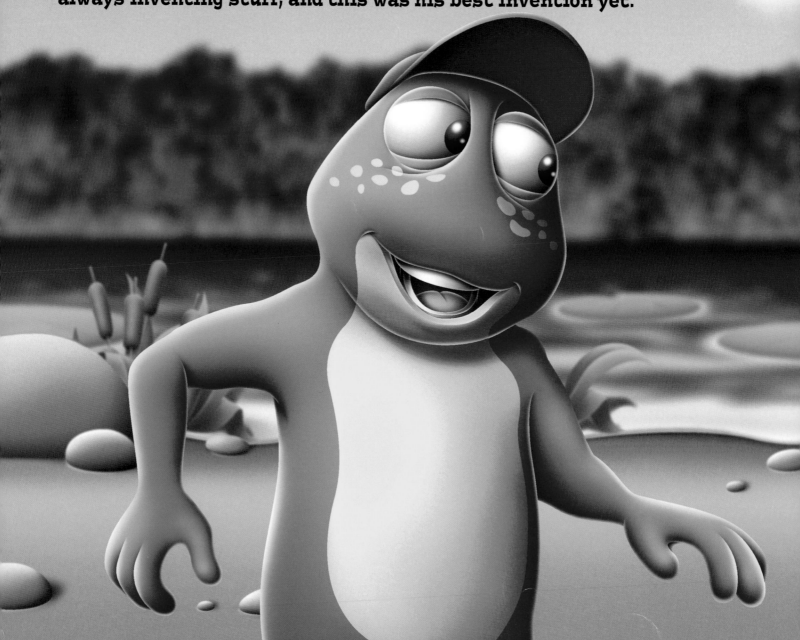

An alligator slowly slithered through the swamp. As it slinked close to the shore, it opened its mouth . . . and a little orange toad hopped out!

Yep, to most folks around Hoppers Landing, this would be a pretty strange sight. But not to Tad. His friend Toad (that's the little orange guy) was always inventing stuff, and this was his best invention yet.

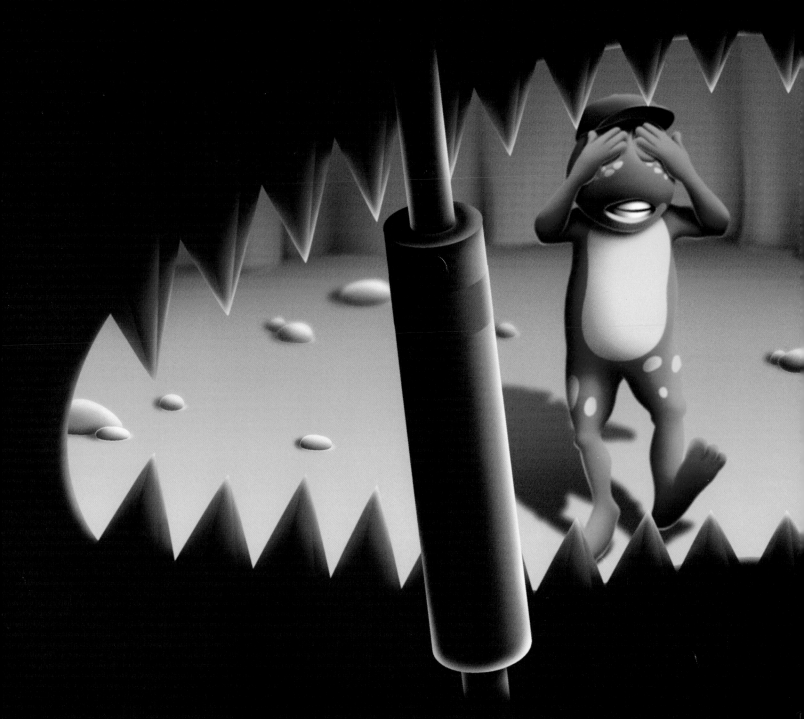

ll aboard!" Toad called.

"I'm coming!" said Tad.

You see, this was no ordinary alligator. This was a boat disguised to look like an alligator. It seemed so real Tad had to close his eyes before he could step inside.

Welcome aboard the Gatorboat!" Toad announced. "It's powered by an inverse propulsion system with—" Toad stopped. "Excuse me, are you listening?"

No, Tad wasn't. There was so much to see! "Toad, this is awesome! Where do you steer this thing?"

"The correct term is the 'bridge.' Just take those stairs and—"

Before Toad could finish, Tad hopped up the steps.

"I'll join you as soon as I hoist the anchor," Toad called after him.

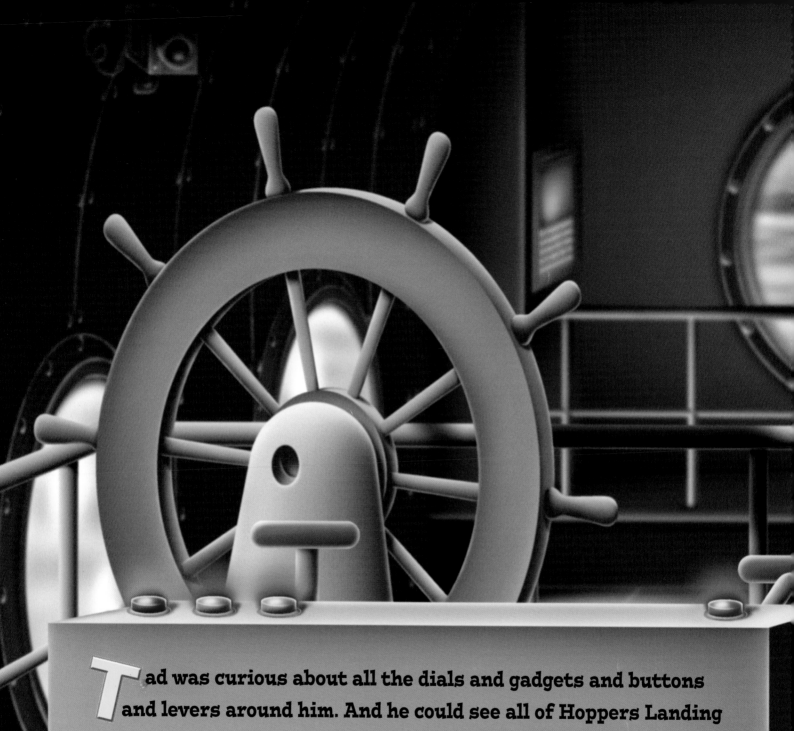

Tad was curious about all the dials and gadgets and buttons and levers around him. And he could see all of Hoppers Landing from up here!

Then he spotted the pilot's wheel. More than anything else, Tad wanted to steer the Gatorboat. But would Toad let him?

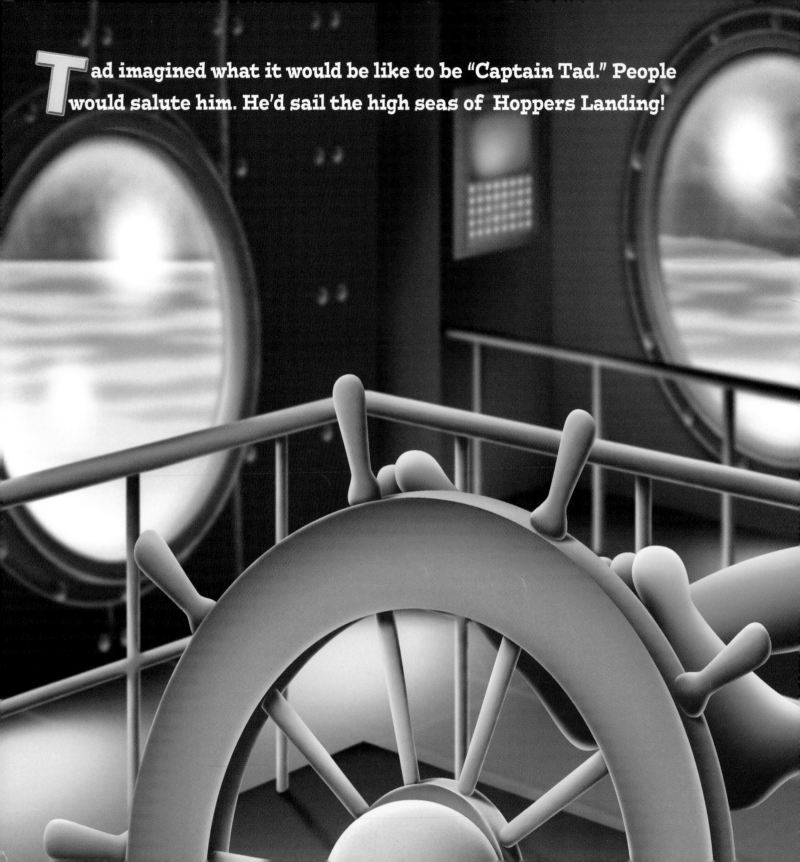

Tad imagined what it would be like to be "Captain Tad." People would salute him. He'd sail the high seas of Hoppers Landing!

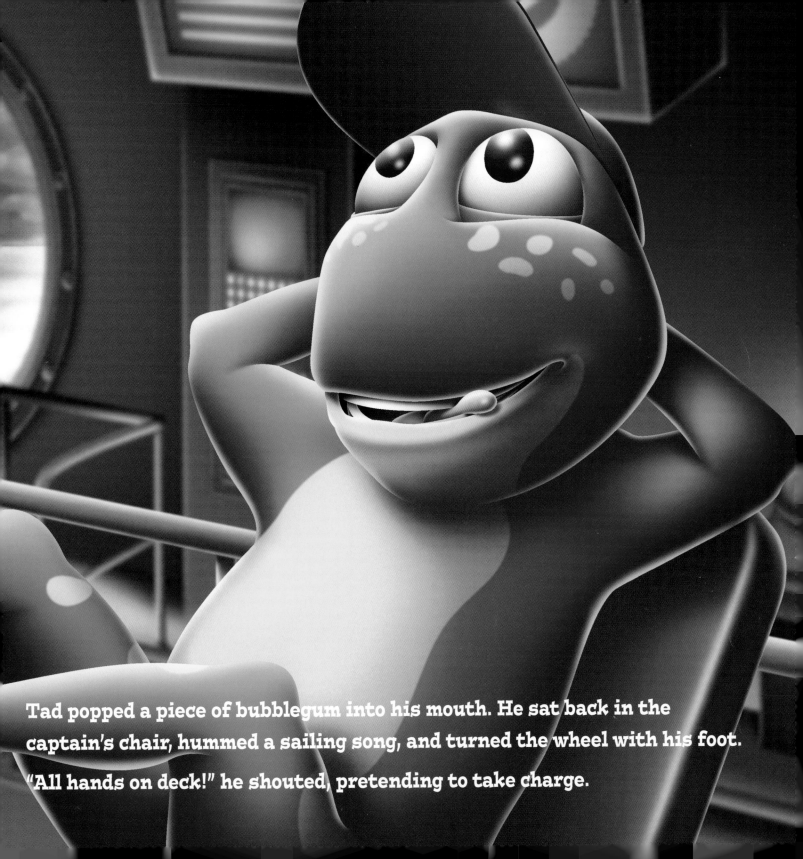

Tad popped a piece of bubblegum into his mouth. He sat back in the captain's chair, hummed a sailing song, and turned the wheel with his foot.

"All hands on deck!" he shouted, pretending to take charge.

Suddenly, the wheel spun around. Tad jumped up to grab it and fell against the controls. Oh no, he broke a lever! What would Toad say?

"You're in trouble now!" hissed a voice. It was ol' Cottonmouth. "You'll never get to steer the Gatorboat if Toad finds out," he said. "You need to hide what you did." Then Cottonmouth disappeared.

Tad didn't trust that old snake. But what he'd said made sense. Maybe he should hide the hole. But how? Toad would be coming back any minute!

Quickly, Tad yanked a crank off the wall and stuck it in the hole—a perfect fit! But that left a hole in the wall! He grabbed a button off the control panel and stuck it in the hole.

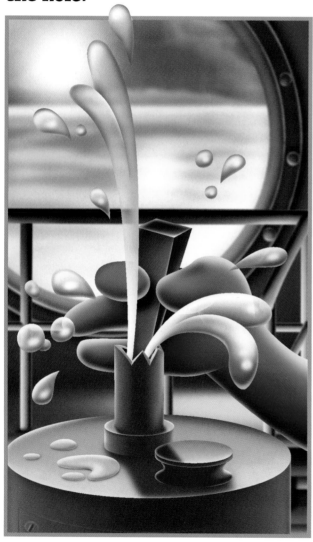

It worked! But now he had a
hole in the dashboard!

Oh no! Toad was coming up
the steps! Tad had an idea.
He took out his bubblegum
and stuck it in the hole.

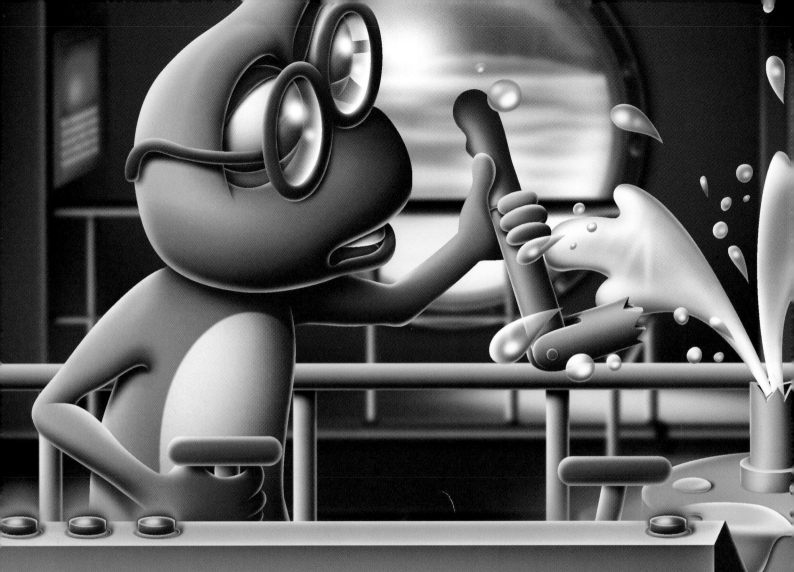

Ready to set sail!" said Toad as he stepped onto the bridge. "Hmm, that's strange," he said, looking at the crank. He shouted out orders. "Get a bearing on the bight below and bridle up the beam!"

"What?" said Tad.

Toad turned the crank. It came loose. "Whoops! Fathom out the fender with the floorboards on the fluke!" Toad cried out.

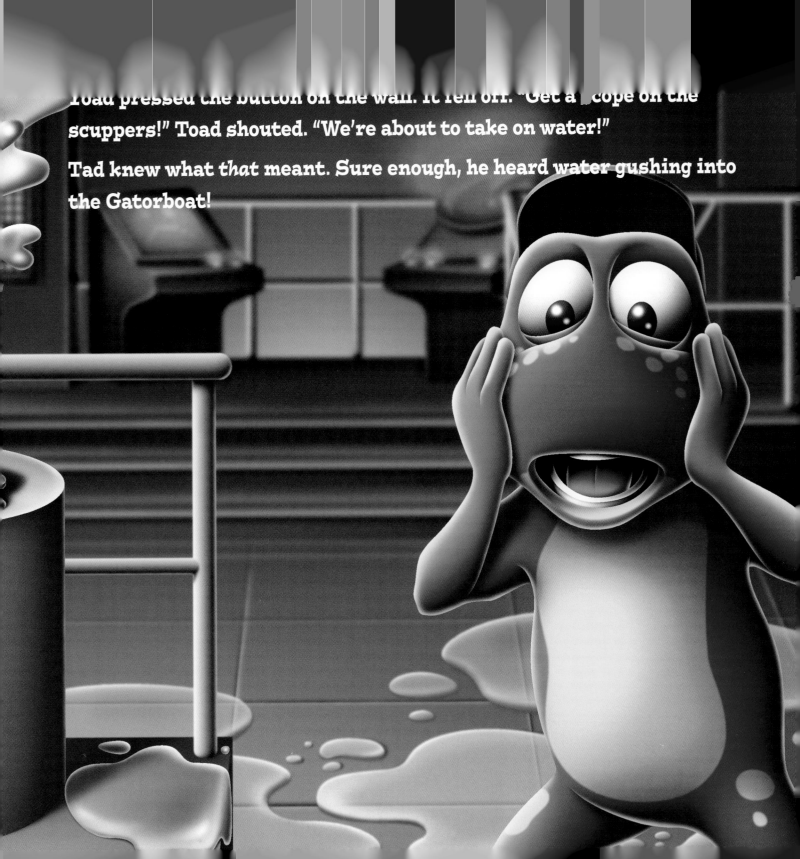

Toad pressed the button on the wall. It fell off. "Get a 'scope on the scuppers!" Toad shouted. "We're about to take on water!"

Tad knew what *that* meant. Sure enough, he heard water gushing into the Gatorboat!

"Don't worry," Toad said, "I'll engage the emergency hatch latch!"
He pushed a button on the control panel. But it wasn't a button at all. He
stared at the piece of bubblegum stuck to his finger.

"It appears
we're in deep trouble,"
said Toad.

Tad felt awful. While Toad hopped around trying to fix everything, Tad looked up. He said a quick, quiet prayer. "God, what should I do?"

Meantime, the Gatorboat was sinking! Tad couldn't take it anymore.

"Toad, I did it!" he cried. "I broke the lever and the crank and the button! It's all my fault!"

Toad looked at his friend. "I was wondering when you would speak up," he said.

"What?" said Tad.

"I saw everything that happened," Toad said, pointing to a camera on the wall. "There really wasn't any danger. I was just hoping you'd tell me the truth."

Tad was embarrassed. "I did tell you the truth . . . but only when I had to. I'm sorry, Toad. I really am. Will you forgive me?"

Of course I forgive you," Toad said. "But next time tell me the truth first—even if it hurts. Okay?"

"Okay," said Tad.

Toad winked. "Now, how about that ride? Only this time, I'll steer."

Toad smiled. Tad grinned back. And off they went for the ride of their lives.